Belinda and the Bears Go To School

Belinda and the Bears Go To School

Kaye Umansky

Illustrated by
Chris Jevons

Orion
Children's Books

ORION CHILDREN'S BOOKS

First published in Great Britain in 2016
by Hodder and Stoughton

1 3 5 7 9 10 8 6 4 2

All characters and events in this publication, other than those clearly in the public domain, are fictitious and any resemblance to real persons, living or dead, is purely coincidental.

A CIP catalogue record for this book
is available from the British Library.

ISBN 978 1 4440 1356 6

Printed and bound in China

The paper and board used in this book are from well-managed forests and other responsible sources.

Orion Children's Books
An imprint of Hachette Children's Group
Part of Hodder and Stoughton
Carmelite House
50 Victoria Embankment, London EC4Y 0DZ

An Hachette UK Company

www.hachette.co.uk
www.hachettechildrens.co.uk

For Freya, Elinor and Reuben

Contents

Chapter One

There were two cottages in Honeybear Lane. One had a door painted green.

Behind that door lived Belinda, with her mum, dad and a cat called Gertie.

Behind the blue door lived...
The Three Bears!

The Bears had come to live in Honeybear Lane when their house in the wood had been knocked down to build a motorway. Goldilocks had made them very nervous of little girls, but they liked Belinda. She was always there when they needed help.

Every morning when Belinda walked to school, she waved to the Bears. Daddy Bear was usually gardening. Mummy Bear was often baking.

Baby Bear was always at the window, waving and waving until Belinda was out of sight.

"What does Baby do all day?" Belinda asked one Saturday.

Baby Bear was doing a handstand.

"Look at me!" he shouted. He loved it when Belinda came round.

"He blows his trumpet up in his room," said Daddy Bear.

"He pesters me for biscuits," said Mummy Bear.

“He races around being a fire engine,” said Daddy Bear.

“Or bounces on his bed.” Mummy Bear sighed. “He’ll break the springs, I know he will.”

“Maybe he’s bored,” said Belinda. “He needs other children to play with.”

“We don’t know any other children,” said Mummy Bear.

"He could come to my school," said Belinda. "He'd have lots of fun, and learn things too."

"Like what?" asked Daddy Bear.

"Like how to write his name and count to ten. And sing songs and draw pictures," said Belinda.

Baby Bear was the right way up now, listening.

"Bears don't go to school," said Daddy. "It's not a Bear thing."

"Why not?" said Belinda. "He might like it. We could give it a try."

Chapter Two

There were only two classes in the village school. Mrs Appleby taught the small children. Belinda's teacher was called Miss Flowers.

The bell had rung and everyone was lining up when Belinda and the Bears arrived on Monday morning.

Daddy Bear was wearing his best hat and scarf. Mummy Bear had her flowery hat on. Baby Bear was wearing his bow tie and waistcoat. All three looked nervous.

The children *gasped* in surprise when they *saw* the Bears. So did the parents at the *gate*.

“Hello, Mrs Appleby,” said Belinda. “These are the Three Bears.”

“Pleased to meet you,” said Mrs Appleby.

If she was surprised, she didn't show it. It takes a lot to surprise teachers.

"Baby Bear wants to come to school," said Belinda.

"Does he?" said Mrs Appleby. She smiled at Baby Bear, who hid even further behind Belinda.

Mrs Appleby turned to the waiting children. “In you go, everyone. I’ll be just a moment.”

Miss Flowers led the children inside.

“So,” said Mrs Appleby to Baby Bear. “Is this your first time at school?”

Baby stared at his feet.

“Answer the teacher, son,” said Daddy Bear.

"He's shy," said Mummy Bear. "Everybody feels shy at first."

Mrs Appleby held out her hand. "Do you want to come and meet the other children, Baby?"

Baby Bear shook his head.

"Here's an idea!" said Mrs Appleby. "Belinda can come and spend the day in my classroom too. I'm sure Miss Flowers won't mind. Would you like that?"

Baby nodded. He took Belinda's hand.

"Don't worry," said Belinda to Mummy and Daddy Bear. "I'll look after him."

Chapter Three

In Mrs Appleby's classroom, the children were having great fun.

Some of them were playing with water.

Some were playing with sand.

Others were drawing pictures, or making things with modelling clay, or pulling toys out of the toy box.

Baby Bear stared.

"What would you like to do first?" Belinda asked.

Baby Bear didn't answer. He had seen a little boy playing with a red fire engine. He loved fire engines!

He let go of Belinda's hand, ran over and snatched it from the boy. The boy gave a wail.

"No!" cried Belinda. "You mustn't snatch!"

But Baby Bear hugged the fire engine close.

Mrs Appleby came over.

"Ben had it first," she explained. "In school, we learn to share. If you ask nicely, I'm sure he'll let you play too. Just say please."

"Peeze?" said Baby to Ben.

"OK," said Ben.

Together, they played with the fire engine.

After that, Baby Bear spotted the water!

He ran over, pushed a little girl out of the way and made a big splash with his paws.

"No, no!" cried Belinda. "You mustn't push!"

"You have to be gentle," said Mrs Appleby. "Say sorry to Jenny. You've wet her dress, see?"

"Sorry, Jenny," said Baby Bear.

And he played nicely.

After that Baby Bear saw the dressing-up box!

A little boy was pretending to be king. Baby snatched his crown and put it on his head.

“No!” cried Belinda. “Give it back!”

"You can be king when Nitan's finished," said Mrs Appleby. "We must learn to take turns."

Baby gave the crown back and waited his turn.

Chapter Four

After that, with Belinda and Mrs Appleby's help, Baby Bear had a good day.

At Circle Time, he sat between Ben and Jenny and drank his milk and ate his biscuit.

At Story Time, he listened quietly. The story was about a naughty monkey who stole bananas. Everyone giggled at the funny bits!

Belinda helped him make a sandcastle in the sand tray. They made a little flag to put on top.

With Ben and Jenny, Baby Bear built a big tower of bricks. Mrs Appleby said it was the tallest she had ever seen!

Just before Home Time, Baby Bear drew a picture of Mummy Bear, Daddy Bear, himself and Belinda.

Mrs Appleby wrote his name on the bottom.

At Home Time, Baby Bear gave Mrs Appleby a big bear hug!

"Would you like to come again tomorrow?" asked Mrs Appleby.

And Baby said,
"Yes, peeze!"

Chapter Five

Daddy Bear and Mummy Bear were waiting outside with the other parents.

Baby Bear ran into Mummy Bear's arms.

"We missed you!" cried Mummy Bear.

"Did you have fun?" asked Daddy Bear.

"Yes," said Baby. "I like school."

"Was he a good boy?" Mummy asked Belinda.

"Very good," said Belinda. "He learned how to share and how to be gentle, and how to take turns. And he made a sandcastle and built a big tower of bricks."

"That's a lot in one day," said Daddy.

"And that's not all," said Belinda. "Show them, Baby."

Proudly, Baby Bear held out his picture.

"That's wonderful!" cried Mummy Bear.

"You can see it's me," said Daddy Bear. "That's my scarf!"

Together, they walked back along Honeybear Lane.

"Did you talk to the other parents?" Belinda asked Mummy Bear.

"We did," said Mummy Bear. "So many people invited us for a cup of tea, didn't they, Dad?"

"They did," said Daddy Bear. "I must say they're making us very welcome."

Belinda gave a happy sigh. Everything was working out perfectly.

Chapter Six

That evening, Belinda lay in bed.

"How was school?" asked her dad, when he came to say goodnight.

"It was fun," said Belinda. "I spent the day in Mrs Appleby's class, helping Baby Bear settle in."

"Baby Bear went to school?" said her dad, surprised.

"Yes. He loved it. And Mummy and Daddy Bear are making friends too," said Belinda.

“Well, that’s good,” said Dad. “I’d like to meet them. So would Mum.”

“They’ve had lots of invitations to tea,” said Belinda. “They’re very popular. But we could invite them on Saturday.”

"Let's do that," said Dad. "We've heard such a lot about these Bears. It's time you brought them round."

He gave her a wink, a kiss, and turned out the light.

Belinda lay back on the pillow. She felt pleased with herself. She had helped the Bears in so many ways. Thanks to her, they were really settling in to village life.

"I think we'll be friends for ever," she told Gertie.

And they were.

MAKE A BOOK

1. Draw a picture of you and your family. Write on all their names.

2. Draw a picture of your teacher.

3. Draw a picture of your best friend.

4. Draw a picture of your pet, or pets.

5. Staple them together.

6. You have made a book!